Saint Germaine
and the Sheep

Saint Germaine and the Sheep

by

Eva K. Betz

Illustrated by

Charles B. Vukovich

Neumann Press
Charlotte, North Carolina

Easy Reading Books of
SAINTS AND FRIENDLY BEASTS

Nihil Obstat:
Bede Babo, O.S.B.
Censor Liborum

Imprimatur:
✝ James A. McNulty
Bishop of Paterson

Saint Germaine and the Sheep

ISBN 978-1-930873-96-4

Printed and bound in the United States of America.

Neumann Press
Charlotte, North Carolina
www.NeumannPress.com
2013

For My Grandson Michael

"Germaine, tell us a story!"

"Tell us about King David and his harp."

"No, I want to hear about the Baby Jesus."

Eleven year old Germaine smiled at the children jumping about her in the field, and sat down on the grass so they could come near her.

"Why not have both stories?" she asked. "But before I begin, you must show me how well you remember your prayers. Say the Hail Mary together, and then we will have the stories."

"Prayers! All the time prayers!" scolded one cross little boy.

But his friends hushed him very quickly.

"It will make Germaine sad if you grumble about saying your prayers," they told him. "And we don't want to make her sad because she is very good to us."

So the children said their Hail Mary, and then they all moved as close as they could to where Germaine was sitting. As she began her story they grew very quiet, and it seemed to them as if the sheep were listening, too.

Germaine Cousin was born in the village of Pibrac, in the south of France, almost four hundred years ago. She had come into the world with a crippled hand, and she had a skin disease that some people said made her unpleasant to look at. But the children of Pibrac did not think so.

To them she looked very lovely, because she was so kind and good. She always had time to mend broken toys. She would help little girls just learning to sew. And best of all, she knew so many wonderful stories.

But Germaine's stepmother did not like her. She made the crippled hand and the skin trouble an excuse to keep Germaine out of the house.

"She must stay away from the baby," said Mrs. Cousin. "He might catch whatever it is she has the matter with her skin."

So Germaine could not sleep in her bed any more.

"She must not eat at the table with us," said Mrs. Cousin. "The sight of her takes away my children's appetite."

Poor Mr. Cousin had married again soon after Germaine's own mother died, hoping to have a better home for his little girl. But his second wife had such a loud voice and such a bad temper that he agreed to anything she wanted. So he gathered some vines and made a bed out of them in the attic for Germaine.

Germaine did not mind. It was quieter there, and at night she could watch the stars and think about God. She loved God very much.

During the day she often ran to the little church in the village for a visit. Some of the unkind people made fun of her for doing it.

"Look at her! She is only pretending to be pious," they said. "The ugly little girl wants us to think she is holy but she isn't. Holy people don't look like that."

But the people of the village were going to learn how wrong they were. The time was coming when they would be very proud because Germaine had lived near them.

Those in the village who were very poor were always glad they had her as a neighbor. She used to go and help them clean their houses, and when they were sick she helped nurse them. Her food was only the scraps left on the table when her own family had finished eating. But such as it was, she shared it. She picked out the largest pieces of bread and bits of fruit to bring to a hungry old woman in the village who had no one else to help her.

One day, as Germaine was going with her basket of scraps, her stepmother saw her.

"Just look at that girl," screamed Mrs. Cousin. "She is stealing our food! Her father works hard to feed his family and Germaine steals it to give away."

Mrs. Cousin ran after the little girl, took her by the shoulders, and shook her roughly.

"Show me what you have in the basket," she said. "Show me the food you are stealing from my home."

She grabbed the basket from Germaine's hand. But when she looked into it, she gasped in surprise. The bits of food had been changed into beautiful flowers of a kind she had never seen before.   Mrs. Cousin said no more about Germaine taking food to the poor. But she looked around for some other way to make the girl unhappy. At last she thought she had found a way.

"Germaine must not sleep in the attic any more," she said. "She makes noise up there and it disturbs me. She'd better sleep out in the barn with the sheep. She is in the field with them all day so she might as well be with them at night, too."

But instead of making Germaine sad, this made her happy. Christ had been born in a stable, and it made her feel very close

to Him to be sleeping in one herself. And, besides, she was fond of the sheep and liked to be with them.

She used to laugh to see the little lambs in the springtime. They looked like toys that had come to life. She also enjoyed watching the ewes, the mother sheep. They were good and kind to their babies but they were strict with them, too. If any of the little lambs did anything his mother thought he should not do, she would ba-a-a a scolding at him. And sometimes she would bump him very hard with her head to punish him. So the little lambs were trained to behave.

The sheep and lambs were about the only playmates Germaine

had. But tending the flock was not merely work, it was fun. Sometimes she would twist flowers in the wool on the old ewe's heads.

"Now you have your best hats on," she would laugh. "You look very nice, I must say. Are you going to a party?"

Sometimes she would run across the fields and the baby lambs would rush along behind her, rocking back and forth on their funny, crooked legs. Then when Germaine stopped, the lambs would stop, too, and look about them as if they were wondering why they had run so far and so fast.

And the mother sheep in their flower hats would ba-a-a as if they

were laughing at their silly children.

There was only one thing that Germaine did not like about being a shepherdess. Now she could not go to Mass in the morning, or get to the church for a visit in the afternoon. The sheep could never be left alone. They might stray and fall into the stream which flowed between the field and the part of the village where the church was. Or even worse, they might wander into the woods where wolves would surely eat them.

But one day Germaine felt that she just must go to church. She gathered the sheep around her and spoke to them.

"I am going to call at God's house," she told them. "He is the Good Shepherd and the Creator. He made me and He made you and He made the grass that you eat."

She took her shepherd's staff and stuck it into the ground in the middle of the field.

"While I am gone," she said, "you must all stay very near this staff. There is plenty of grass for

you here and you cannot get into trouble. And while you are near the staff the wolves will not come out of the woods, even though I am not here."

The sheep looked at her quietly and she felt that they understood what she had said to them. So she ran down the hillside, and over the little plank bridge across the stream, and on through the village to the church. She said her prayers and talked to God in the Tabernacle for a while. Then she said good-bye to Him and

hurried back to her flock once more.

The sheep and lambs were quietly cropping the grass around the staff that Germaine had set in the ground. None had fallen into the river nor had the wolves come to bother them. But as soon as she pulled the staff from the ground, the sheep scattered. The blac-knosed lambs scampered off, twitching their tails, and rocking from front hoofs to back, and sometimes jumping high in the air with fun and excitement. Their yellow-eyed mothers were more sedate. But even they seemed glad to be able to wander a little farther.

Germaine was very happy to know that it was possible for her to go to church. Every day, after that, she would try to get to Mass, or at least to make a visit to her Friend in the Tabernacle. She would plant her staff firmly in the ground, tell the sheep that they must stay near it, and then go off without any worry about the flock.

The village children some-times came for their stories while Germaine was gone. They were surprised to see the sheep in a circle around the staff. But they did not mention the strange thing to their

parents because so many of the
grown people did not like Germaine.

The boys and girls kept
coming back until they found her.
They loved her stories, and many
of them learned all they knew of
God and His Commandments
from the tales she told them.

The summer passed, and
the lambs lost their dark baby
wool and grew white and fat like
their mothers. Autumn winds
blew. Then winter reached its icy
fingers into the barn and pinched
Germaine where she lay trying to
sleep. When she shivered a little
in the cold, the sheep moved near

her and lay with their heavy wool against her. Then she smiled and grew warm and fell asleep.

And so it went, year after year.

Germaine would sleep in the sheep barn. When daybreak came, she would take the sheep into the fields and set up her staff to protect them while she went off to Mass.

Sometimes in the spring she would weave wreaths of the bright flowers and give them to Our Lady for a crown. In summer, when she ran down for an afternoon visit at the church, she often brought a nosegay as a gift for the Friend Who waited for her there. And

always, when she was gone, the sheep would remain near her staff, obediently waiting for her to come back and set them free to wander. It was plain that they loved their shepherdess very much. And year after year, as new families of lambs came along, they learned from the older ones how to behave while Germaine was gone.

Then came a very cold winter, a worse one than even the oldest man in the village could remember. The streams all froze, and heavy snow fell, and it was hard for the sheep to find

enough grass to eat. Mr. Cousin even bought a little hay for them although his wife did not like to spend the money. But she did not scold too much about it. She had grown much kinder than she used to be. She did not speak sharply to Germaine so often, and she gave her more and better food to eat. Mr. Cousin, too, was kinder to his little girl.

He told her she could come into the house and sleep in the little bed that used to be hers. But she asked to be allowed to stay in the barn. The Baby Jesus had been born in a stable, so she liked to sleep in one. When He grew to be a Man, He had died on a wooden cross, so she liked to lie on the wooden floor.

She continued to spend her nights with the gentle sheep. She took good care of them, and they did their best to take care of her and please her.

The winter stopped and spring came very suddenly, with warm nights and hot days. Streams thawed, ice and snow melted, and the water ran down the hillsides and poured into the stream. The water level rose so high, and its current went with such a rush, that it carried away the planks of the bridge. Poor Germaine!

"How can I get to the church now?" she wondered. "It may be a long time before the men get around to mending this bridge—if they ever do."

There was another crossing much farther up the stream but it would take Germaine too long to go that way. The bridge now destroyed had not been used by many people of the village, so she was sure that the men would not be in a hurry to repair it. She felt very sad indeed to think that perhaps she would no longer be able to get to Mass or even to visit the church. Then one morning when

it seemed to her that she could wait no longer, she set her staff in the field as she used to do. The sheep obediently gathered around it and she walked away from them and down the bank that rimmed the water.

The stream was very wide now with all the water from the hills, and was racing along fast. When it dashed against a rock it jumped up in white spray. When it came to smaller stones it tumbled

and rolled them along like small cannonballs. And it had grown very deep, too much deeper than it had ever been before.

A branch torn from a tree came rushing down the stream, carried along at a great rate. The twigs spread out like hands and seemed as if they were trying to catch Germaine's skirt and pull her along. She knew that if she fell in the water she could not get out again because the current was so strong. But she did not run away. She just stood at the edge of the stream a moment. Then she stepped into the water.

As she did so, the waters parted and she got safely across.

The next morning on her way to Mass, the same thing happened. But this time there were some children on a hill nearby and they saw the strange event.

"Did you see that?" a big girl said. "She stepped right into the rushing water. It is running so fast it could knock a man down!"

"It didn't knock Germaine down," said her little sister. "When she got across her skirt wasn't wet, not even her shoes were wet."

"I don't understand it," said a boy.

The littlest boy spoke up.

"It seemed as if when she stepped into the river there wasn't any water where she was," he said.

This time the children did run home and tell their parents what they had seen. But no one believed them.

"What nonsense!" said one woman.

"You are making up stories," said another. "Children must be punished for not telling the truth."

Later in the day the women met at the market place and began talking about the silly things their children were saying about Germaine.

"They say she walked right into the raging water," said one woman.

"And that the water parted to let her get across perfectly dry," added another.

"And they say, now, that for a long time she has been coming to the church every day and leaving her shepherd's staff to mind the sheep!"

But the mother of the smallest boy now spoke up.

"My little son has never told me a lie," she said. "He did see

something strange this morning. I am sure of that."

The other women stared at her.

"Well, what do you think he saw?" they asked.

"I don't know. But tomorrow I am going to get up very early. I'll hide behind the bushes on the hill and see for myself what goes on."

"We will go with you," said the other women.

So the next morning, very early, the women climbed the hill beside the stream. They saw Germaine come out with her sheep, and saw the sheep scatter about the field and begin to graze.

But, as Mass time drew near, they saw Germaine push the end of her staff into the ground. And when she did, the sheep all moved up close to it and began grazing there.

"You'd think that there was a fence around them," whispered one of the women.

Then Germaine climbed down the bank toward the rushing stream. It was wilder than ever this morning because there had been a heavy rain the night before.

"Oh, I hope she doesn't try to wade across," said one woman. "I have never liked the child much but I wouldn't want to see her drown."

"She will surely be knocked

down and drowned," added another.

"Let us watch and see what happens," said the smallest boy's mother.

When Germaine got to the edge of the water, it stopped its wild rush. A path opened up for her and she walked across without getting her skirts wet or even her shoes.

"The girl is a saint!" the women said.

They hurried back to the village and went to Mass, although usually they went only on Sundays.

The people called her a
saint, although she didn't know
it. It would have made her very
unhappy if she had. The mothers
were glad to have their children
go and sit in the fields and listen
to Germaine's stories of Mary and

her Son. She was twenty-two years old, now, and over the years she had taught many children their prayers and told them of the love of God. Both the lambs and the children grew up but there were always new ones to take their places.

One morning Mr. Cousin went into the kitchen for his breakfast.

"I don't know where Germaine is," his wife said. "I had a packet of bread and cheese for her to take to the fields when she went with the flock. But she didn't come in to get it."

"She probably forgot all about it," said Mr. Cousin. "She thinks so much about her prayers that she is likely to forget everything else. I'll take it to her."

But when he got to the meadow where the flock was supposed to be grazing, it was empty. Neither Germaine nor the sheep were in sight.

"This is very strange," Mr. Cousin said to himself. "I never knew her to be late in taking out the flock. She has always been a most dependable girl."

He hurried up the hill and around the house to the big barn. He threw open the door, and there was his daughter lying on the floor, smiling sweetly as if she saw something very lovely.

The sheep were standing motionless, their heads hanging sadly. One little lamb was licking Germaine's hand as if trying to warm it. But Germaine did not know that. Her soul had gone to heaven with the Good Shepherd and she would not take this flock out to pasture any more.

Her family and the people in the village all knew, now, that a

very wonderful person had died. They buried her inside the parish church and her family were very sad that they had been unkind for so long to the girl. But, after a while, many of the people forgot all about her.

Forty years later one of her cousins died. She was to be buried in the grave with Germaine. When they opened the grave they found Germaine's body unchanged, her smiling face looking just as it had long ago. Now all the village knew that a saint had lived there.

In the parish at that time there lived a wealthy woman. She was very sick and the doctors could do nothing to cure her. She had a new little baby son who was sick, too, and when she asked the doctors if he would get better they just shook their heads sadly.

So the woman prayed to Germaine. She asked the shepherdess to speak to God for her.

"Ask Him to let my little boy live," she prayed. "And ask Him to make me better so that I can care for my baby."

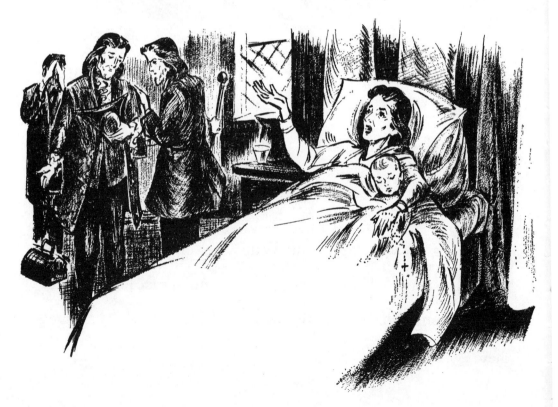

Suddenly the mother and the baby boy were both well and strong.

"We did not cure them," the doctors said. "It was something besides our medicine that made this woman and her child well."

When the story became known, more and more people began to ask Germaine to speak to God for them. Blind people asked for the return of their sight. Crippled people asked that they might walk again. And God gave to many, many of them the miracles they asked for.

In 1845 there was a convent of Good Shepherd nuns in France who were having a hard time. They had very little food, but they did not mind this for themselves. It was the poor girls they were caring for who worried them. The people depended on the Sisters and they could not be allowed to starve. So every day the Sisters ate less and less. But still there was not enough.

Then they began to pray to Germaine.

"She was a shepherdess," they said, "and she took good care of her sheep. She will surely be willing to speak for us Sisters of

the Good Shepherd, and ask God to help us feed our flock of unfortunates."

They prayed very hard. And suddenly it seemed as if the food they had was multiplied. What had looked like too little was enough to feed all the girls and the Sisters, and there was always some left over!

Finally the priests and bishops wrote to the Pope.

"We think this young shepherdess was a saint," they said. "Wonderful things have happened to people who have asked her to pray to God for them."

Letters came from all over the world telling about miracles which had been brought about through Germaine's intercession. And finally, in 1867, Pope Pius IX said that Germaine was indeed a saint.

When you see pictures of her she is sometimes shown making thread from the wool of her sheep. Or she may be shown with a basket of flowers, to remind us of the time the bread was changed to flowers to save her from a scolding. But usually you see pictures of Saint Germaine with the sheep, the kind animals she loved and who loved her.